Mallory Cox and his
Magic Socks

Andrew Matthews
Illustrated by Tony Ross

J.M. Dent & Sons Ltd
London

First published in 1990
Text copyright © Andrew Matthews 1990
Illustrations copyright © Tony Ross 1990
All rights reserved

Printed in England
for J. M. Dent & Sons Ltd
91 Clapham High Street
London SW4 7TA

British Library Cataloguing in Publication Data
Matthews, Andrew, *1948–*
    Mallory Cox and his magic socks.
    I. Title   II. Ross, Tony, *1938–*
    823'.914[F]

ISBN 0–460–88011–X

For Doris, Elizabeth and Tony

-1-

A Great Aunt from Up North

Mallory Cox was a know-it-all and a show-off. When other children at school tried to tell him anything, he blinked his eyes behind his big, round spectacles and said, "Didn't you know that? I knew about it ages ago!" in a loud voice. Mallory's voice was maddening. It was like a pair of hobnailed boots that trampled over everyone. Even teachers got trampled by Mallory's hobnailed boot voice.

"If you ask me," he said in lessons, "this isn't proper teaching at all! I read all this in my encyclopaedia ages ago! I thought school was supposed to tell us about things we didn't know!"

Hardly surprisingly, Mallory had no friends. He was not popular with the other children at school, or the teachers; in fact his own parents got fed up with him at times.

Mallory didn't have any toys and didn't play any games. There were no story books or comics in his bedroom. Mallory liked to read books with titles like *The Giant I-Bet-You-Didn't-Know-That Book* and his favourite hobby was fiddling about in the garden shed. He had taken apart a lot of old lawn mowers and radios and spent hours sticking bits of them together. When his parents asked what he was doing, he replied, "Well, it's obvious, isn't it? I'm building a robot. Its name is Mallory One!"

To tell the truth, Mallory didn't have the faintest idea how to build a robot – though he would never have admitted it, of course. His parents knew he didn't have the faintest idea about robots, but they didn't admit it either. It was more peaceful having Mallory fiddling about in the garden shed than have him hanging around the house, telling them things they didn't want to know until their heads ached.

One evening not long after Mallory's ninth birthday, he was seated at the work-bench in the garden shed reading the *Ginormous Know-It-All Book For Boffs*. He was so fascinated by the chapter he was reading – "Fifty Facts your

Teacher won't know about Dinosaurs" – that it was some time before he noticed that a storm was raging. Rain fell in sheets, pillow cases and duvet covers. Lightning zipped across the sky and thunder crashed like enormous marbles being rolled over an even more enormous tea-tray. The wind howled round the shed like a starving werewolf.

"If you ask me, the weather's taken a turn for the worse!" Mallory said to himself.

Suddenly, between peals of thunder, Mallory heard a noise like a cackling laugh coming from far off.

"Someone likes the rain, anyway!" he said.

Another giant rumble of thunder grumbled through the clouds and when it died away, Mallory heard the cackling laugh again, sounding much closer this time. All at once there was a BAM! BAM! BAM!-ing on the shed door that made the whole place shake. It went on and on and on.

"Hmm!" said Mallory. "If you ask me, someone wants to come in!"

When he opened the door, Mallory found himself facing the most extraordinary old woman he had ever seen. She wore ragged clothes and a tall, pointed black hat with a wide brim. The point of her long, curved, warty nose almost touched the tip of her long, curved, warty chin. Her eyebrows were as bristly as a pair of hedgehogs and her hair looked like grey spaghetti. She pointed the handle of a broomstick at Mallory.

"Ey-up! You're Mallory!" she screeched. She let fly a laugh like two cats fighting in a pile of rusty tins.

"I know," said Mallory calmly. "I found that out ages ago!"

The old woman peered suspiciously round the shed and pointed her broomstick at a heap of junk on the work bench.

"What's that, when it's at home?" she asked.

"That's going to be my robot. I'm going to call it the Mallory One!"

"Fancy, now!" smiled the old woman. "Well, I'll have you know that I'm your Great Aunt Enid from up North and I've come to see you. Are you going to invite me in?"

Lightning crackled and thunder crashed at her words.

"Um ..." said Mallory, rather wishing the old woman would stay outside in the rain.

"Well, there's gratitude for you!" snapped the old woman. "I've flown all the way to see you and give you your birthday present! Still, if you're not interested ..." she half-turned away.

"Perhaps," said Mallory, his eyes shining greedily, "perhaps you could come in for a minute."

The old woman stepped over the threshold and shook the rain off her clothes. A huge black bat wriggled down one of her sleeves and fluttered off into the storm.

"Did you have a good flight?" asked Mallory.

"Thunder and lightning all the way!" beamed the old woman. "I love a good tempest! It's so good for the skin! There's nothing to beat being up there, riding a broomstick through the lashing wind and hail!"

Mallory's eyes opened wider than the

mouths of a pair of yawning walrus.

"You ... er ... mean you flew on a b-broomstick?" he quailed.

"Aye!" the old woman nodded vigorously. A tarantula spider fell off the brim of her hat and went scuttling off across the floor.

"And ... er ... you didn't fly in an aeroplane?" asked Mallory.

"Aeroplane?" jeered the old woman. "Tish and tosh! Aeroplanes are for namby pambies!"

Mallory suddenly felt as though his knees had turned into chocolate mousse.

"If you ask m-me," he said slowly, "it sounds as though you're some kind of witch!"

"Some kind?" bristled the old woman. "How many kinds of witch are there, then? As far as I know there's only one sort of witch, and I'm it! Take it or leave it, please yourself!"

Mallory sat down in an old deck-chair and scratched his head.

"But there's no such thing as witches!" he protested. "It said in my encyclopaedia that witchcraft was just a lot of old nonsense!"

"Ee! Fancy that, now!" growled the old woman. She clapped her hands. There was a flash of blue light, and a clay pipe appeared out of nowhere. The old woman put the stem of the pipe into her mouth and began blowing figure of eight smoke rings. "If there's no such thing as witches, then there's no such thing as me," she said. "No, and no such thing as your birthday present, either!"

"What is the present?" asked Mallory.

The old woman leaned close and spoke in a hoarse whisper.

"Summat special! It's a present I made you myself – and a fiddly job it was too, I can tell you! I had to find all the makings myself and if I told you half the things I went through to find them, it would make your hair stand in on end!"

"You mean up on end," Mallory corrected her.

"I mean your hair would be so frightened, it would shrink back into your head to hide!" said the old woman.

"Bet it wouldn't!" gulped Mallory.

The old woman reached up, lifted her hat and produced a small parcel wrapped in flowery paper tied with a bow of blue ribbon.

"There, lad!"

Trembling with excitement, Mallory took the parcel and unwrapped it. When he saw what was inside, his mouth fell open and his forehead wrinkled up like a crinkle-cut crisp.

"B-but ... it's a pair of socks!" he wailed. "A pair of grey, woollen socks!"

"Aren't they champion?" giggled the old woman. "I made them grey specially. Grey's my favourite colour, you know!"

Mallory stared, disappointed. The socks looked all too ordinary to him. He couldn't understand why the old woman had made such a fuss about them.

"Thanks very much," he mumbled, "they're just what I always wanted. Only, you needn't have come all this way yourself. You could have posted them."

"Posted them?" screeched the old woman. "And risk having them lost?"

"If you'd sent me a postal order, I could have bought myself some socks," said Mallory.

"No you couldn't, lad!" rasped the old woman. "Those socks of yours are magic! They don't look anything special, but when they start working..." She winked and clicked her tongue, "Ecky thump!" The old woman reached under her hat again and drew out an hourglass. "Ee! Just look at the time! I shall have to be on my way! There's a big witches' 'do' on up North and I mustn't be late!"

"But, Great Aunt Enid!" spluttered Mallory. "How are they – what do they – I mean, when will they – ?"

"Just wear 'em, lad!" said the old woman. "You're a Cox, and that means there's magic in you that wants bringing out! Now, I must fly, so you'd better stand well back! I'm not as young as I used to be and I've got to take a bit of a run at it!"

With those words, the old woman raced off into the belting rain. Mallory peered into the darkness, and by the light of a bolt of lightning, glimpsed his Great Aunt Enid soaring off over the rooftops, waving farewell.

Mallory didn't know what to think. For a long time he looked at the socks and then he folded them carefully, put them in his pocket and went into the house to see his parents. Mr and Mrs Cox were in the lounge. Mrs Cox was watching television and Mr Cox was doing a crossword.

"Mum," said Mallory, "Dad, have I got a Great Aunt up North?"

"Yes," said Mr Cox.

"Is her name Enid?"

"That's right," said Mrs Cox.

"Oh!" said Mallory. "And is she a witch?"

Mr Cox looked up from his crossword with a troubled look on his face. "A witch?" he repeated. "Well ... since you've brought the matter up, yes, she is a bit on the witchy side. But why do you want to know?"

"She brought me a pair of magic socks," said Mallory. "She said magic runs in our family."

"It does," said Mr Cox. "Trouble is, no-one knows what direction it's going to run in!"

"How very interesting!" said Mallory, and went straight off to bed.

- 2 -

Another Great Aunt

When Mallory woke the next morning, he took a long look at the socks his witchy Great Aunt had given to him. In daylight they looked even more ordinary than he remembered. It was very disappointing. Mallory put on his dressing gown and slippers and stumped sulkily downstairs.

His parents were reading newspapers over breakfast, and neither of them looked up when Mallory appeared.

"If you ask me, this magic lark is nothing but a big swizz!" Mallory announced loudly. "I've got a pair of socks that are supposed to be magic, but they look pretty boring to me!"

"These things take time, Mallory," observed Mr Cox, turning a page of the newspaper.

"You must learn to walk before you can run!"

"Your socks are a very peculiar colour, dear!" said Mrs Cox, peering under the table at Mallory's ankles.

"I'm not wearing any socks!" protested Mallory.

"Perhaps you should," said Mrs Cox. "Maybe the magic won't start working until you put them on."

"Of course!" Mallory muttered to himself. "I should have thought of that!" He muttered very quietly, so that his parents wouldn't hear him. "I must pop upstairs for a minute," he cried.

Mallory forgot what his father had said about walking before he could run and went racing upstairs faster than a scalded baboon.

With shivery hands, he picked the socks up from his bedside table and slipped them on.

At once, his feet began to tingle and tickle as though the socks had cold electric ants wriggling around inside them. Mallory looked down at his feet and gasped. The socks weren't grey and ordinary any more. They were incredible! They were staggering! They were outrageous! They were covered in sparkling blobs, shiny squiggles, shimmering stars and silvery crescent moons. There were shapes that looked like the letters of some crazy language, shapes that looked like numbers and other shapes that looked like nothing on earth.

"Crikey!" croaked Mallory. "Crumbs! What's happened to my socks? I must show Mum and Dad at once!"

As Mallory crossed his bedroom on the way to the door, he caught sight of himself in the mirror. His hair was bright purple!

"Gosh!" squeaked Mallory. "Golly!" The surprise made his hair turn orange and then pink as he got more used to the idea of having hair as colourful as a mandrill's bottom. Mallory thundered downstairs, making as much noise as an army falling out of bed.

"Mum! Dad! Look at me!" he cried.

His parents were in the front hall. Mr Cox
was just about to leave for work and Mrs Cox
was waiting to kiss him good-bye.

"I see," said Mr Cox calmly.

"Oh dear!" exclaimed Mrs Cox, raising the
back of her hand to her mouth in alarm. "I'm
not sure that glowing yellow hair suits you,
Mallory!"

"Isn't it pink any more?" said Mallory
regretfully.

"It's all right!" said Mr Cox. "It's gone dark
green now!" He frowned sternly at Mallory.
"No school for you today!" he said.

"Oh, pooh!" grumbled Mallory, his hair turning maroon. "I wanted to show my wacky hair off to the teachers and the other kids!"

"Sparkling blue hair is only the start, Mallory," said Mr Cox gravely. "Now the magic has begun to work, who knows what might happen? It's far too dangerous for you to be at school!"

"What's dangerous about school?" asked the now lavender-haired Mallory.

"Nothing, so long as you don't go," replied Mr Cox. "I don't mean that you would be in danger, I mean the school would be at risk from your magic! And now, I must dash. I mustn't be late for work!"

After Mr Cox had left, Mrs Cox looked at Mallory and her face went pale. His hair was like Neapolitan ice-cream.

"Mallory!" she croaked. "Your head is making me feel quite ill! I'm going upstairs to lie down!"

"All right!" said Mallory. "I'm going to make myself a gooseberry jam and peanut butter sandwich, then I'm going down to the garden shed for a good old fiddle about!"

After eating his sandwich, Mallory got dressed and went out into the garden. His hair was traffic-light red as he stepped out of the back door. Unfortunately none of the neighbours was out in the garden to catch sight of him.

Before he reached the end of the garden path, Mallory could see that there was something terribly wrong with the shed. The door was wide open and the inside was a complete mess – jam-jars had been smashed on the floor and shelves had been knocked down. It looked as

though a herd of rhino had used the shed as
a disco.

"If you ask me, this is all very strange!"
Mallory said aloud. "It wasn't like this when
I left it last night! Everything was neat and
tidy! It looks like a burglar has been in here
looking for something. I wonder wha–?"

Mallory broke off suddenly as he heard
noises behind him. There was a bumping, a
buzzing, a clattering and a scratchy voice
which said, "So there you are! About time you
turned up!"

Mallory wheeled around and found himself staring at a junk sculpture in the shape of a person. It had two glowing radio dials for eyes and a loudspeaker for a mouth. Its body was made of lawn-mower wheels and a tin bucket. A spade and an old rake served it as arms. With a start, Mallory realised that it was his robot and that his magic socks had been at it again.

"But –" he stuttered. "But-but-but!"

"Hmm!" said the robot. "Sounds like you need oiling!" It rattled close to Mallory, raised its rake left arm and squirted something into Mallory's wide-open mouth. It tasted terrible! Mallory coughed and spat.

"Are you trying to poison me or something?" he gasped.

"Nonsense!" retorted the robot. "I just dosed you up with cod-liver oil! Do you the world of good! Now then, are you ready?"

"Ready for what?"

"Things to do, my boy, things to do!" barked the robot. "This shed wants sorting out for a start. Garden wants looking at, too! The lawn could do with a trim and those rose-trees need cutting back. After that, you can get some ladders and brushes and start painting the outside of the house!"

"Just a minute!" frowned Mallory. "This can't be right! I thought robots were supposed to do the work while people gave the orders!"

"Work?" cried the robot. "Me? With my incredible know-how? I'm far too valuable and delicate to do any work, lad! I might get fluff in my circuits, and then where would we be, eh?"

There followed two long, hard-working hours. Following endless instructions from the robot, Mallory swept and dusted and scrubbed and polished until the inside of the shed gleamed. He was more than grateful when the robot allowed him to take a ten-minute break.

"Of course," it said, "you haven't given the place what I'd call a proper clean, bless me, no! To get this shed looking really spick and span..."

The robot chuntered on until Mallory's head span.

"Just my luck!" he muttered. "I get a pair of magic socks and what happens? I get hair that goes every colour of the rainbow and a bossy robot that thinks it's a world expert on everything!"

He picked up his *Ginormous Know-It-All Book* and started looking through the section on dinosaurs he had been reading the previous evening. Just at that moment something peculiar happened. A small black hole appeared in one of the walls of the shed. It was like looking down a long dark tunnel. Somewhere far off Mallory could see a tiny figure astride a tiny broomstick. The figure was waving, frantically trying to draw attention to itself.

Mallory stared, open-mouthed, as the figure grew larger and larger until it stood, life-sized, on the floor of the shed in front of him. It was a withered crone, wearing a tall black hat and ragged clothes. She pointed a crooked finger at Mallory.

"At last!" she shrilled. "I've got you now and there's no escape! I want what was stolen from me back right now!"

"I'm very sorry," said Mallory. "I don't know what you're talking about!"

The robot rattled over to stand beside Mallory. "That's the way, lad!" it muttered encouragingly. "Play dumb!"

"I'm talking about stolen property!" screamed the crone.

"Who are you?" Mallory demanded, his hair turning the colour of peas mashed up in tomato sauce. "What gives you the right to appear in my shed and accuse me of stealing things?"

The crone raised her right hand in a sinister way, then paused and appeared to change her mind. She stretched her mouth into a smile that looked as cheerful as a ruined castle on a drizzly day.

"Me?" she cooed. "Why, I'm your Great Aunt from up North, chook!"

"No you're not!" said Mallory. "I've met my Great Aunt from up North. Her name's Enid and you're nothing like her?"

"I'm your *other* Great Aunt, you great soft pudding!" snapped the crone. "Great Aunt Gussie! Enid's my sister! I might have known she'd be at the bottom of all this! She's always been jealous of me!" Great Aunt Gussie leaned close to Mallory and put on a revolting wheedling voice. "Don't you want to help your poor old Great Aunt get back what's rightfully hers?"

"Don't trust her, lad!" wheezed the robot.

"Well –" said Mallory. "Er –!"

Great Aunt Gussie shrieked with rage. She

wrenched the *Ginormous Know-It-All Book* from
Mallory's hands, intending to hit him over the
head with it; but when she saw the dinosaur
pictures a sly smile spread over her face.

"Very well!" she crowed. "Let's see if a little
spell won't make you more co-operative! Let's
see how you like being sent back to the time
of the Thunder Lizards!"

"Watch out, lad!" cried the robot.

It trundled in front of Mallory as the witch
raised her left hand. A ball of blue fire engulfed
Mallory and the robot, and as Mallory stared
with terrified eyes the shed and the garden
began to fade. The colour drained out of them
and something else began to show through,
growing clearer by the second.

- 3 -

In the Jungle

Mallory and the robot found themselves standing in the middle of a jungle clearing. It was a funny-looking jungle. The trees were tall and thin with scaly bark and long, feathery leaves. The air was warm and filled with wispy steam so that sunlight came through the branches of the trees in misty bars. Frogs in colours as bright as Mallory's hair hopped about on the soggy ground and dragonflies the size of seagulls droned through the shadows.

"What's going on?" protested Mallory. "I don't like the look of this place one bit! Where are we?"

The robot clicked and whirred. Lights flashed inside its head.

"Same place, different time, lad. That nasty old Great Aunt of yours has sent us back about 142 million years, give or take a million." Totally unconcerned, the robot clanked its way over to the nearest tree, prodded at a vine with its spade arm and tutted disapprovingly.

"Shocking!" it said. "Once you let a place go like this, you may as well dig the whole lot over and start again from scratch! And just look at this grass! Some people don't know the meaning of the word lawn-mower."

"But ... if we've gone back that far," shivered Mallory, "we're in the time of the dinosaurs, aren't we?"

"Quite right!" replied the robot. "Fascinating stuff, eh? Look and learn, lad! That's my

advice to you! You seem keen on finding out
about things."

"I used to be keen, now I'm not so sure,"
Mallory confessed.

"He-llo!" said the robot curiously. "Don't
look now, but we're being watched!"

Trembling with fear, Mallory turned his
head. No more than three metres away, at the
edge of the clearing, stood a small dinosaur.
It was less than a metre long and most of that
was tail. Its skin looked smooth and shiny and
was dark grey, with bands and patches of green
that made it blend with the background. The
dinosaur stood on its long back legs and stared
with yellow eyes that glittered in its tortoise-
shaped head.

"I didn't know there were little dinosaurs as well!" whispered Mallory.

"Look and learn, lad!" said the robot. "Got anything to eat on you?"

"I'm not hungry, actually," replied Mallory.

"I didn't mean for you! If you feed this little chap, you might be able to make friends!"

Mallory pulled a bar from his pocket and looked at it regretfully.

"I've only got this crispy Harvest Chew," he said. "I was saving it to keep up my energy-level throughout the morning – but still – if it's in the interests of science –"

The dinosaur became quite interested in the chew bar. When Mallory removed the wrapper, the little creature cocked its head to one side. When Mallory broke a small piece off the end, the dinosaur made a ticking sound in the back of its throat.

"Want some?" coaxed Mallory. "There you go then!"

He threw the piece of chew bar into the air. The dinosaur sprang for it in a flicker of grey and yellow and its jaws closed with a snap like an elastic band.

"Well that's not a very good way of eating!" said Mallory. "You're supposed to chew food properly before you swallow it! No wonder you all died off!"

Before Mallory could throw a second piece of chew bar, something startled the small dinosaur. It flashed off into the dark of the deep jungle faster than the eye could follow.

"I wonder what frightened it off?" Mallory mused sadly.

The robot made a whistling sound.

"Er, hello!" it said. "Don't look now, but we're being watched again!"

The air was torn apart by a crashing and cracking. The ground trembled. Something behind Mallory let loose an enormous, hissing roar and he turned to look. His hair went lime green. A fearsome, six-metre-tall dinosaur was striding through the jungle towards the clearing, shattering trees as it came. The great scythe of its tail smashed down bushes and saplings. Each step it took made the earth shake. It roared again, showing a forest of long, sharp fangs.

"Er ... tell me," gibbered Mallory, "is it a plant-eating dinosaur?"

"No, lad," replied the robot. "That's a *Tyrannosaurus rex*, the biggest meat-eating animal that ever lived."

"I was afraid it might be!" boggled Mallory. "What shall we do?"

"If you take my advice, you'll run as fast as you can that way." The robot pointed away from the *Tyrannosaurus*. "Head for that pile of boulders. I think I can detect a cave!"

Mallory could see the boulders in the distance. They were round and grey, like a heap of deep-frozen elephants. Mallory took a deep breath and ran. He belted through bushes, flew through ferns and pelted through pools of swampy water. At school, he didn't pay much attention to sport, but it didn't show now. If someone had been present with a stop-watch and a tape measure, Mallory would have been declared Junior Champion in sprinting, hurdling and long-jumping. If there had been records for somersaulting and scrambling over rocks, Mallory would have broken those as well. In no time at all, he was crammed into a cave in the boulders where it felt cool and dark and safe. Outside, the robot clanked and clattered towards the cave with the *Tyrannosaurus* close behind.

"Come on! Faster!" cried Mallory.

"It's no use, lad!" called the robot. "I was never intended for speed, you know! Maybe the *Tyrannosaurus* isn't an adventurous eater!"

But it seemed that the robot was wrong. The monster had caught up with the robot, and bent forward to enclose it in its slavering jaws. The robot lifted its left arm and let fly a hefty squirt of cod-liver oil that went straight down the dinosaur's throat. The *Tyrannosaurus* straightened up, working its jaws like a dog chewing a toffee. A glazed look came into its eyes, and it shook its head and spat.

Mallory was amazed when the *Tyrannosaurus* began to twitch and ripple all over like the top of a boiling porridge pot.

"It's shrinking!" he exclaimed.

The dinosaur was not only shrinking – it was changing shape and colour. Mallory just had time to catch a hint of ragged clothes and tall black hat before everything started to fade.

"Here we go again!" he groaned.

- 4 -

A Magic Duel

The inside of a cottage replaced the jungle. It was a particularly dark and dreary cottage. Rickety chairs were piled high with books and parchment scrolls and bunches of dried plants dangled from low, black beams in the roof. A chart showing the signs of the zodiac hung from a mildewed wall. On a table below the chart a glass flask of red liquid bubbled and smoked. Beside the table stood Great Aunt Enid. She had obviously just returned from the big witches' 'do', because there were party streamers dangling from her black hat and she was holding a broomstick with tinsel wound around the handle.

"Ey, up, Mallory, lad!" she cackled. "I found you just in time!"

Mallory blinked in astonishment and his hair went turquoise.

"Where's my robot?" he asked.

"Right here!" said the robot, popping into view beside him. "And I think someone else we know is going to arrive at any second!"

Great Aunt Gussie appeared out of nowhere. She was clutching her throat and her tongue was stuck out.

"Cod-liver oil!" she gasped. "Ugh!"

She ran over to the flask of red, bubbling liquid and drank it down in one gulp.

"That's better!" she sighed. She stared around the cottage with narrowed eyes. "It's a plot!" she screamed in a voice like fingernails scraping on slate. "A vile, wicked plot!"

"No it isn't!" said Mallory faintly.

"Then what was he doing with you in that garden shed?" demanded Great Aunt Gussie, pointing at the robot.

"It's my robot," Mallory explained. "I made him. Sort of."

"Made him?" scoffed Great Aunt Gussie. "The only thing you could make is a nuisance of yourself! Can't you see it's not a robot at all, you great soft lump!" She waved her hands through the air. A ball of white light appeared above the robot's head and came slowly down over it. The robot quivered and started to melt. With a final flicker of white light, it changed into a portly black cat.

"There!" said Great Aunt Gussie trium-
phantly.

"Aye!" sighed the cat. "It looks like the jig's
up!"

"Who are you?" gasped Mallory. "Don't
tell me you're a Great Aunt as well!"

"Nay, lad," the cat replied. "Stalleybrass is
the name. I belong to your Great Aunt Enid.
And Gussie's quite right, it is all a vile, wicked
plot! Your Great Aunt Enid turned me into
a robot so I could keep an eye on you."

"But –" blurted Mallory, "what – how –
why –"

"Enid," the crone demanded sternly, "what
did you do with my balls of dragon's wool,
you sneaky sister?"

"Dragon's wool?" puzzled Mallory. "But
I thought dragons were covered all over with
scales!"

"They are," said Stalleybrass. "That's why
dragon's wool is so magic."

"I'll tell you what I did with your precious
wool!" growled Great Aunt Enid. "I used it
to make something useful, instead of just
gloating over it like you used to!"

"Rotten thief!" cried Great Aunt Gussie.

"Well at least I don't turn myself into a dinosaur and go terrifying innocent children!" Enid retorted.

"But what did you make my wool into?" bawled Gussie.

The truth dawned on Mallory like a shower of cold water and made his hair turn the colour of fish fingers.

"She knitted me a pair of socks for a birthday present!" he exclaimed.

Great Aunt Gussie's eyes bulged in outrage.

"Socks!" she hissed. "You mean Enid took eight balls of the finest dragon's wool and turned them into a pair of socks for a little squirt like you?"

"It's too late to fret about it now!" said Great Aunt Enid. "I've given Mallory the socks and their magic belongs to him. I did it for the good of the family name!"

"Ooh!" sulked Great Aunt Gussie. "You're that big a liar, our Enid! You stole my dragon's wool because you were jealous! You've always been jealous of me because I'm a wickeder witch than you are!"

The light of battle gleamed in Great Aunt Enid's eyes.

"Right!" she said, rolling up her sleeves. "We'll soon see who's wickeder! Take that, you daft old bat!"

There was a loud BLAT! and a puff of evil-smelling smoke. When the smoke cleared, a huge toad stood where Great Aunt Gussie had been.

"You saucy trifle!" croaked the toad. "Put that in your pipe and smoke it!"

There was a loud BLOT!, another cloud of smoke and Great Aunt Enid changed into a scraggy-looking chicken.

"You spiteful ratbag!" clucked the chicken. "See how you like that!"

BLOOT! went a cloud of smoke and the toad turned into a jar of instant coffee.

"Think that's wicked?" rattled the jar. "Well let me show you something ..."

Stalleybrass the cat cleared his throat and brushed Mallory's leg with his tail. "If I were you, lad, I'd be off home," he advised. "Last time those two had a row like this, it went on for fifteen years."

"But how can I go home?" whinged Mallory.

"Just hop on that broomstick over there and fly home!" said the cat. "Your magic socks will protect you!"

There was nothing else for it. Mallory gingerly made his way around the two Great Aunts (now a green jelly rabbit and a battered copper kettle) and picked up the broomstick with tinsel wrapped around it.

"Where to, guv?" asked the broomstick.

"My house," said Mallory. "Better make it the garden shed."

"No sweat!" said the broomstick. "'Ang on tight, an' if you don't like 'eights you better keep your eyes shut!"

When Mallory dared to open his eyes
again, he was safe at home in the garden
shed.

"Thank goodness all that's over!" he sighed.
"I must take off these pesky socks before
something else happens!"

As soon as Mallory took off his socks, they
went back to being grey and ordinary, and
his hair went back to normal. Mallory was
hungry and it was too chilly to stay in the
shed without any socks on, so he went into
the house.

His parents were in the kitchen. Mr Cox, wearing a frilly pinafore, was scrambling eggs in a large saucepan while Mrs Cox was busy with the crossword in the evening paper.

"Your head's back to its usual self, I see, Mallory," said Mr Cox.

"Yes!" said Mallory. "I've taken off those dratted socks and I never want to know anything about magic ever again!"

"Thought so," said Mr Cox. "I decided the same thing when I was your age. I bought

you a present to take your mind off it!"

"Here you are, dear," said Mrs Cox, handing over a paper bag. Inside the bag was a large book, whose title was *The Thick Heavy Book Of Really Big Meat-Eating Dinosaurs*.

"Oh, pooh!" cursed Mallory. "I don't want to know anything about dinosaurs either! In fact, I'm fed up with knowing things all the time! I think I'll stop showing off and have a nice quiet life instead!"

"Quite right!" said Mr and Mrs Cox.

Despite what he had said about the socks, after he had gone to bed that night Mallory couldn't resist putting them on just once more to see what colour his hair would go.

"Only raspberry-ripple coloured!" Mallory said to himself, looking into the wardrobe mirror. "That's not very interesting!" While he

waited for his hair to change into something
more spectacular, Mallory started to read a
book he had taken out of the library, *The Boff's
Book Of Pirates*.

"Hmm!" he said aloud. "I wonder what it
was really like on board a pirate ship in the
Spanish Main . . ."

Before the words were out of his mouth, the magic socks started to tingle and glow. The walls of Mallory's bedroom turned misty. He heard the faint sounds of creaking timbers, crashing waves and men singing sea-shanties. The sounds grew louder as he listened.

"Oh dear!" exclaimed Mallory. "I wonder if I'll have to walk the plank?"